Mr. and Mrs. Muddle

MARY ANN HOBERMAN
CATHARINE O'NEILL

Joy Street Books
Little, Brown and Company
Boston · Toronto

For Julian from Ama
—M.H.

For my father
—C.O'N.

Library of Congress Cataloging-in-Publication Data

Hoberman, Mary Ann.
Mr. and Mrs. Muddle / written by Mary Ann Hoberman;
illustrated by Catharine O'Neill.
p.   cm.
Summary: Mr. and Mrs. Muddle, a horse couple, have to learn to
compromise on the one thing they don't agree on.
ISBN 0-316-36735-4
[1. Horses—Fiction.]   I. O'Neill, Catharine, ill.   II. Title.
III. Title: Mister and Mistress Muddle.
PZ7.H6525Mr   1988
[E]—dc19   87-27320
                                                    CIP
                                                    AC

10 9 8 7 6 5 4 3 2 1

HOR

Published simultaneously in Canada
by Little, Brown & Company (Canada) Limited

Printed in the United States of America

CHAPTER 1

The Riddle

Mr. and Mrs. Muddle were married.

Most of the time they liked the same things.

They both liked bread and butter and baseball.

They both liked telephones and telescopes and television.

But there was one thing they could not agree on.
Mrs. Muddle liked cars.
Mr. Muddle hated them.

Mrs. Muddle loved nothing more
than going out for a drive.
Mr. Muddle would rather walk.

It was a problem.

"Let's go for a ride,"
Mrs. Muddle would say hopefully.
"Let's go for a walk,"
Mr. Muddle would reply.
So they wouldn't do either.

"Aunt Bessie has invited us to dinner," Mrs. Muddle would say happily.
"She lives too far away," Mr. Muddle would answer.

So they wouldn't go.

"Let's take a walk to the store for some ice cream," Mr. Muddle would say hungrily.
"Let's drive," Mrs. Muddle would reply.

So they stayed home.

It was nice being home together.
But going out together would have
been nice, too.

"Let's ask Elmer for advice," said Mr. Muddle.
"He knows everything."
"Nobody knows everything," said Mrs. Muddle.
"But Elmer does know quite a lot.

"Let's drive over to his house to ask him,"
Mrs. Muddle suggested.
"Let's walk there," said Mr. Muddle.
"Let's telephone," said Mrs. Muddle.
"You're so smart," said Mr. Muddle. "If only
you didn't like cars so much, you'd be perfect."
"Where shall we meet him?" asked Mrs. Muddle.
"Let's ask him to come here," said Mr. Muddle.

"You're so clever," said Mrs. Muddle. "If only you liked cars, you'd be perfect, too."
"Nobody is perfect," said Mr. Muddle.
"But it's nice to come close."

CHAPTER 2

The Middle

Elmer came over.

"What's the matter?" he asked.

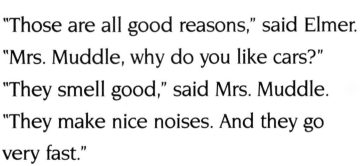

Mr. and Mrs. Muddle told him.
"That *is* a problem," said Elmer.
"Mr. Muddle, why don't you like cars?"
"They smell," said Mr. Muddle.
"They make noise. They go too fast."

"Those are all good reasons," said Elmer.
"Mrs. Muddle, why do you like cars?"
"They smell good," said Mrs. Muddle.
"They make nice noises. And they go
very fast."

"Those are all good reasons, too," said Elmer.
"Let me think for a while."

Finally he was done.
"You are right," he said to Mr. Muddle.
"And you are right," he said to Mrs. Muddle.
Mr. and Mrs. Muddle looked at each other.
"How can we both be right?" they asked.
"Sometimes it happens," said Elmer.
"But if we are both right," said Mrs. Muddle,
"then where is the answer to our problem?"
"If you are both right," said Elmer,
"then the answer must be somewhere in the middle."

"What's in the middle of a ride and a walk?"
asked Mrs. Muddle.
"What's in the middle of cars and feet?" asked Mr. Muddle.
"Think," said Elmer.

"How about a pogo stick?" said Mr. Muddle.

He loved pogo sticks.

"Pogo sticks use feet," said Mrs. Muddle.

"How about a scooter?"

"Scooters have wheels," said Mr. Muddle.

"How about a . . ."

"Boat!" shouted Mrs. Muddle, jumping up and down.

"That's just what I was going to say!" said Mr. Muddle.

"It was on the tip of my tongue."

"Cars aren't everything," said Mrs. Muddle.

"Feet aren't everything," said Mr. Muddle.

"Glad to be of help," said Elmer.

CHAPTER 3

The Puddle

Mr. and Mrs. Muddle bought a canoe.

They named it *Puddlejumper*.

They painted the name on the side in red letters.

They carried Puddlejumper to a big puddle
near their house.

The puddle was muddy.

"Ugh!" said Mrs. Muddle. "I hope we don't tip over."

"Don't worry," said Mr. Muddle. "I know how to paddle."

They got in.

It felt very tippy.

"Maybe I should paddle, too," said Mrs. Muddle.

"No," said Mr. Muddle firmly.

He put his paddle in the puddle.

The canoe began to move.

"Oh, this is fun!" said Mrs. Muddle.

"Wake me up when we get to the other side."

Mr. Muddle kept on paddling.

"Are we there yet?" asked Mrs. Muddle.

But Mr. Muddle did not answer.

Mrs. Muddle opened her eyes.

"We're going around in circles!" she said.

"I thought you knew how to paddle!"

"I do," said Mr. Muddle.

"Let *me* try," said Mrs. Muddle.

She took a paddle and put it in the puddle.

"We're moving!" she said.

"We're moving in a circle the other way,"
said Mr. Muddle.

"Oh, dear!" said Mrs. Muddle. "You're right.
I wonder what's the matter?"

"Is something wrong?" someone said.

It was Elmer. He was swimming in the puddle.

He did not mind mud.

Mr. and Mrs. Muddle told Elmer their problem.

"When I paddle on my side,"

said Mr. Muddle, "we go around one way."

"And when I paddle on my side," said Mrs. Muddle,

"we go around the other way."

Elmer thought for a long time.

"The answer is somewhere in the middle," he said finally.

Then he swam away.

"He always says that," said Mrs. Muddle.

"What is in the middle this time?" asked Mr. Muddle.

"That we *both* paddle?" answered Mrs. Muddle.

"Let's try it!" they said together.

Mr. Muddle took his paddle and paddled on his side.

Mrs. Muddle took her paddle and paddled on her side.

"We're moving straight ahead!" said Mr. Muddle.

"Hooray!" shouted Mrs. Muddle.

"Stop bouncing up and down!" cried Mr. Muddle.

But it was too late.

"Swim to shore!" yelled Mr. Muddle.

"Swim to shore!" Mrs. Muddle yelled back.

So they did.

"You're on the wrong side," called Mr. Muddle.
"Come over here."
"No, you are," Mrs. Muddle called back.
"You come here."
Neither of them moved.
"*Please* come here," said Mrs. Muddle.
"Please come *here*," Mr. Muddle replied.
They still stayed where they were.

"I'll swim halfway if you swim halfway," called Mr. Muddle.

"All right," called Mrs. Muddle.

So they each swam halfway.

And they met in the middle.

They turned *Puddlejumper* over and climbed inside.
And they paddled home to lunch, side by side.

$13.45